W9-BKH-520

I Want It All!

I Want It All!

By Barbara Ciletti

Illustrated by Cathy Morrison

Columbus, Ohio

This edition published in 2006 by Gingham Dog Press, an imprint of School Specialty Publishing, a member of the School Specialty Family. Printed in South Korea. Previously published in special edition by Terra Publications, a division of the Ciletti Publishing Group, Inc. 2421 Redwood Court, Longmont, CO 80503.

Library of Congress Cataloging-in-Publication Data is on file with the publisher.

Send all inquiries to:
School Specialty Publishing
8720 Orion Place
Columbus, OH 43240-2111
ISBN 0-7696-4376-0
1 2 3 4 5 6 7 8 9 10 PAC 10 09 08 07 06 05

Dedicated to children
young and old,
who realize
that the greatest
gift of Christmas
is not under the tree,
but in the heart.

This is a story

for

Advent.

It tells of the adventures

of a bug called

Moresy

and the lessons

learned by a young boy

named

Benjamin Getts.

When we are children (and even as adults),
we can sometimes forget about the true meaning
of Advent. Its historic beginnings will help us remember.

Every year as Advent draws near, the world
awaits the Feast Of The Nativity.
In the east, shepherds look to the heavens and remember
an event that quietly changed the world
more than two thousand years ago.
After centuries of waiting,
God fulfilled His promise of a Messiah.
Jesus was born.

Around the world, Advent is a season of prayer, of giving and waiting to celebrate the coming of the Lord.

It is also
a season
of song, family
tradition
and eager
anticipation
for the joy
that comes
with
Christmas
Day.

One Advent, not so long ago,
everyone in the Getts family
(or almost everyone) got into the spirit of giving.

Benjamin's mom and dad began to decorate
their home for the holidays.
Gran filled food baskets for poor families.
Gramps cut extra firewood for a neighbor.

Benjamin was busy, too.
He was making a list of gifts, and all of them were for him!
In fact his list was already twice as long as last year's list—
and he was just getting started!

Mom said, "Benjamin, Christmas is a time to receive gifts—yes!
But most of all, this is a time to appreciate what we already have,
and to think of how we can share that with others.
This is the season when we think about giving, not just getting.
Have you thought of what you might like to do
for your sister Kate, for instance?"

"Why should I?" Benjamin grumbled. "Kate already plays with all of my toys. She even gets as many pancakes as I do at breakfast! This time I want more toys for me, and she isn't going to play with them!"

Just then, Gramps walked into the kitchen.
"Hey, buddy! I've got some firewood ready to deliver.
I thought we could take it over on the sled
and then give you and Kate a ride back home.
Sound like fun?"
"Yes!" said Kate.
But, Benjamin wasn't interested.

"Thanks, Gramps, but I really want
to work on my wish list."
Gramps gave Ben a long look.
"Okay, buddy. Just be careful of the bug."

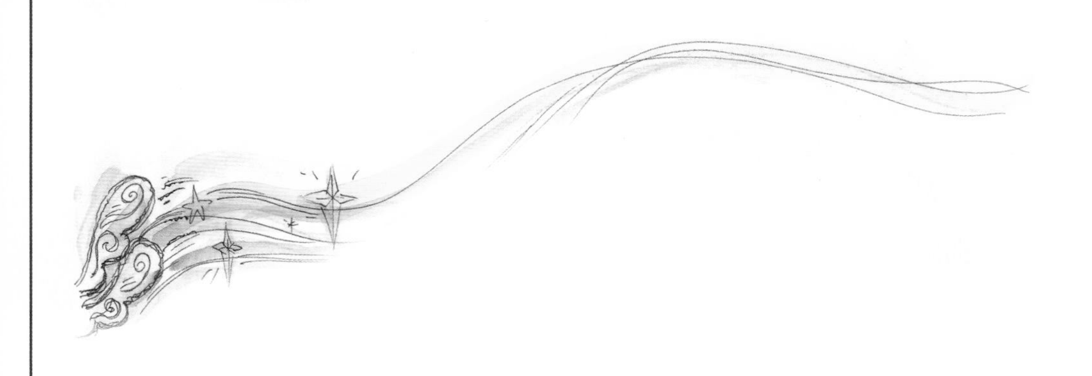

Benjamin worked on his list again that night.
"I wonder what Gramps meant about a bug. Oh well, I'll just ask him tomorrow."

I WANT IT ALL !

The next morning, Ben was brushing his teeth and almost thought he saw a big bug flying around in the bathroom. He blinked, but it was gone.

Later on that evening, Ben climbed into bed and gazed at the sky outside his window.

Christmas morning was just a few days away, and he kept thinking of the trucks, the basketball, and all of the new toys he wanted.

And then, he thought for sure, he saw some sort of bug again.

"Boy I must be really tired. Better get some sleep...."

The next morning, Ben awoke to the sound of something moving in his room. He opened his eyes to the scariest, creepiest bug he had ever seen in his life! And it was looking right back at him!!!

Ben ran into the kitchen where
Gramps was having coffee.
"Gramps! Help!

There's a monster
in my room!"
Gramps eyes twinkled.
"That so?
What does it look like?"

"It's B I G!
With a green speckled body and wings and these
huge blue eyes – just looking at me!"

"Buddy, the Moresy Bug found you.
It comes alive during the Christmas season
and bites people who are never satisfied
with what they have,
people who want more,
and more, and more.

That's how the bug got its
name, but it's pretty much
another word for greed,
and it looks for selfish
people so that it can
be with its own kind."

"How can I make it
go away?"
Asked Ben.

"There's no bug spray for Moresy Bug. You can't chase it off. But, if you start to appreciate your family, our home and all the great gear that's already up in your room, you might have a chance. Better still, work on the list of presents you want to GIVE instead of GET and Moresy will be gone in a hurry."

Ben trailed back to his room.
He felt scared, and sweaty and very alone.
The thought of seeing the Moresy Bug again
made him sick to his stomach.

Ben picked up his list:
A bicycle—well he already had one.
A new computer—why? He had one of those, too.
Roller blades—same thing.
He thought of the first Christmas—
Baby Jesus had NOTHING and He changed the world.

Then Ben did something rather surprising.

He threw his list away.

The next day, Ben went with his dad to deliver cookies to the neighbors. He even helped Kate with a puzzle.

That night, he looked for the Moresy Bug everywhere. Under his bed. Outside the window. No Moresy!

The last few days of Advent passed quickly
And when Christmas Eve finally arrived,
Ben felt warm and happy inside.

He especially hoped that Kate would like her present.
She loved to play with his favorite steam engine.
Ben cleaned it up and painted "Kate" on the side of the car....

Moresy Bug was long gone.

Christmas morning dawned and Ben's family celebrated Christmas services and then went home to open presents. Ben glowed as he watched mom, dad, Gran and Gramps, and especially Kate open the gifts he made for them.

Gramps spied Ben.
"How's it going Buddy?
Get rid of that bug?"
"Yes! I feel much better.
Gramps? Thanks.
This is the best
Christmas ever !"

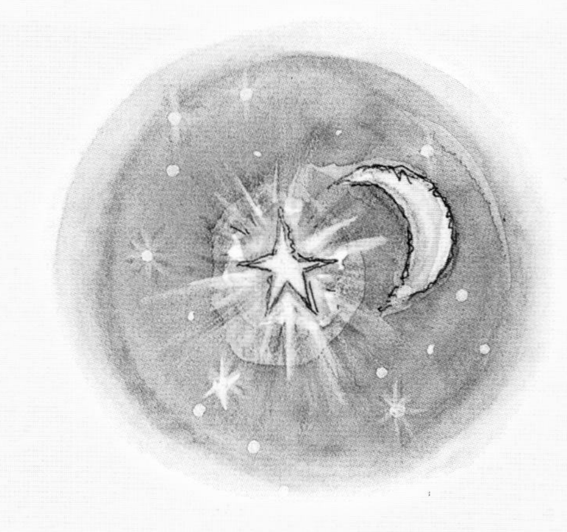

Benjamin's cure for Moresy Bug Bites:

Think about the first Christmas

and be

joyful for your life!

Don't lie awake

with lists you make

in the dark hours of the night.

Moresy Bug

will take the hint

and find someone

else to bite!